For Jo, with all my love.
T. B.

To Sam.
R. B.

This edition published by Parragon in 2012
Parragon
Chartist House
15-17 Trim Street
Bath BA1 1HA, UK
www.parragon.com

Published by arrangement with Meadowside Children's Books
185 Fleet Street, London, EC4A 2HS

Text © Tony Bonning 2004
Illustrations © Rosalind Beardshaw 2004

Printed in China

Kiss the Fr♥g

Tony Bonning • Rosalind Beardshaw

PaRragon
Bath · New York · Singapore · Hong Kong · Cologne · Delhi
Melbourne · Amsterdam · Johannesburg · Shenzhen

Beside a grand and
majestic castle was a pond,

and at the bottom
of this cool, clear pond
lived Snog the Frog.

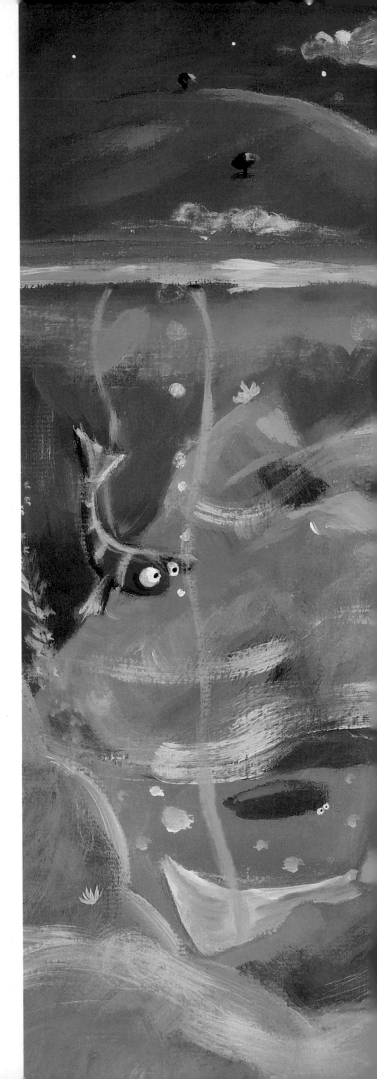

Snog the Frog climbed on his log and said,
"Today is Valentine's Day, and today I wish to
feel like a prince. And to be a prince I need a kiss!"

With that in mind, he leapt onto the land and went

HOPPITY HOPPITY HOPPITY HOP,

until who should he meet, but Cow.

"Oh Cowy Cow Cow! I wish to feel like a prince.
Pucker up your lovely lips and give me a kiss!"

"Who? You? Moo! No! Now go!"
"Oh! Just one?"
"No, go!"
And with that he went . . .

HOPPITY HOPPITY HOPPITY HOP,
until who should he meet, but Sheep.

"Oh Sheepy Sheep Sheep! I wish to feel like a
prince. Pucker those luscious lips and give me a kiss."
"Me? Meh! Baa! Nah! No!"
"Oh! Perhaps a peck?"
"Nooo, go!"

So with that, Snog the Frog went

HOPPITY

HOPPITY

HOPPITY HOP,

until who should he meet,
but Snake.

"Oh Snakey Snake Snake! I wish to feel like a prince.
Press those lean lips on mine and give me a kiss."
"A kiss, hissss, take this!"
"Oh no! I'll give that a miss."

And with this, he went HOPPITY HOPPITY HOPPITY HOP, until who should he meet, but Pig.

"Oh Hoggy Hog Hog give this Froggy Frog Frog a big wet kiss."
"What! Snort! I'd never kiss your sort."
"Spoilsport."

And with that, Snog the Frog went
HOPPITY
HOPPITY
HOPPITY HOP,

until who should he meet, but . . .

...Princess!

"Oh Princess, Your Highness, such happiness would I possess
were you to kiss me but once. Make me feel like a prince."
"Oh!" said the Princess, "I've read about this in the Fairy Tales.
One kiss and you turn into a prince."

And with this, she lifted Snog the Frog
and gave him a kiss.

"Alas, something is amiss.
The kiss has not turned you into a prince."
"Again, again, just one." The deed was done but . . .

nothing!

"Oh my!
Have one last try."
She did.

"I have tried once
and twice more since,
but you have not
become a prince."

"No!"
said Snog the Frog . . .

"But I feel like a prince...
and that's the main thing!"